Books By
RATHER FUNNY PRESS

Would You Rather? For 6 Year Old Kids!
Would You Rather? For 7 Year Old Kids!
Would You Rather? For 8 Year Old Kids!
Would You Rather? For 9 Year Old Kids!
Would You Rather? For 10 Year Old Kids!
Would You Rather? For 11 Year Old Kids!
Would You Rather? For 12 Year Old Kids!
Would You Rather? For Teens!
Would You Rather? Eww! Yuck! Gross!

To see all the latest books by
Rather Funny Press just go to
RatherFunnyPress.com

YOUR FREE SURPRISE GIFT!

HILARIOUS JOKES FOR CLEVER KIDS!

RATHER FUNNY PRESS

To grab your free copy of this brand new, hilarious Joke Book, just go to:

go.RatherFunnyPress.com

Enjoy!

RatherFunnyPress.com

HOW TO PLAY

This easy to play game is a ton of fun!
Have 2 or more players.
The first reader will choose a 'Would You Rather?'
from the book and read it aloud.
The other player(s) then choose which scenario
they would prefer and why.
You can't say 'neither' or 'none'.
You must choose one and explain why.
Then the book is passed to the next person
and the game continues!

The main rule is have fun, laugh and enjoy
spending time with your friends and family.
Let the fun begin!

ATTENTION!

All the scenarios and choices in this book are
fictional and meant to be about using your
imagination, having a ton of fun and enjoying this
game with your friends and family.
Obviously, DO NOT ATTEMPT any of these
scenarios in real life.

RatherFunnyPress.com

WOULD YOU RATHER...

HAVE A SWIMMING POOL IN YOUR LIVING ROOM

OR

A HOT TUB IN YOUR BEDROOM?

GIVE UP PLAYING VIDEO GAMES FOR A MONTH

OR

GIVE UP WATCHING MOVIES & TV FOR A MONTH?

WOULD YOU RATHER...

TRAVEL THE WORLD FOR A YEAR

OR

GO TO THE INTERNATIONAL SPACE STATION FOR A MONTH?

HANG OUT WITH YOUR FAVORITE CELEBRITY EACH WEEK

OR

NEVER HAVE TO DO HOMEWORK AGAIN?

WOULD YOU RATHER...

MEET A PUPPY THAT WALKS ON TWO LEGS

OR

A PUPPY THAT TALKS?

EAT A ROTTEN FISH AND JELLY SANDWICH

OR

EAT A COCKROACH AND CHOCOLATE SANDWICH?

WOULD YOU RATHER...

ALWAYS SNEEZE LOUDLY WHEN YOU WALK INTO A ROOM

OR

ALWAYS SNEEZE LOUDLY WHEN YOU MEET SOMEONE NEW?

HAVE A PET GIANT CRAB YOU CAN RIDE TO SCHOOL

OR

A PET GIANT KANGAROO THAT CAN TAKE YOU TO SCHOOL IN HER POUCH?

WOULD YOU RATHER...

HAVE A PERSONAL LIFE-SIZED ROBOT

OR

A JETPACK?

HAVE EYELASHES SO LONG NO-ONE CAN SEE YOUR FACE

OR

NOSE HAIRS THAT WERE SO LONG THEY DRAGGED ON THE GROUND?

WOULD YOU RATHER...

TAKE A CODING CLASS

OR

AN ART CLASS?

HAVE YOUR CURRENT PET LIVE AS LONG AS YOU DO

OR

BRING A PAST PET BACK TO LIFE?

WOULD YOU RATHER...

HAVE THE HEAD OF
AN ANT

OR

THE BODY OF AN ANT?

SAVE A PRINCESS FROM A
DRAGON GUARDING A CASTLE

OR

KICK THE PRINCESS OUT AND
ENJOY A SWEET NEW CASTLE
AND PET DRAGON?

WOULD YOU RATHER...

KNOW THE HISTORY OF EVERY OBJECT YOU TOUCHED

OR

BE ABLE TO TALK TO ANIMALS?

SUFFER FROM SPONTANEOUS SHOUTING

OR

UNPREDICTABLE FAINTING SPELLS?

WOULD YOU RATHER...

BE A CHARACTER IN FROZEN

OR

A CHARACTER IN STAR WARS?

GO TO YOUR FIRST DAY AT A NEW SCHOOL IN YOUR GRANDMA'S CLOTHES

OR

DRESSED LIKE A BABY IN DIAPERS?

WOULD YOU RATHER...

JUMP INTO FREEZING WATER

OR

RUN ACROSS HOT PAVEMENT?

HAVE FREE WI-FI WHEREVER YOU GO

OR

BE ABLE TO DRINK UNLIMITED FREE COFFEE AT ANY COFFEE SHOP?

WOULD YOU RATHER...

SLEEP ON THE SIDEWALK
FOR A MONTH

OR

SLEEP ON THE ROOF OF YOUR
HOUSE FOR 3 NIGHTS?

KNOW WHAT HAPPENS IN EVERY
MOVIE BEFORE YOU SEE IT

OR

ONLY WATCH MOVIES THAT ARE
A YEAR OLD?

WOULD YOU RATHER...

GET FAMOUS SLOWLY AS A MOVIE ACTOR

OR

GET FAMOUS QUICKLY AS A REALITY TV STAR?

HOLD A SNAKE

OR

KISS A JELLYFISH?

WOULD YOU RATHER...

HAVE AN ARM WRESTLING MATCH WITH YOUR MOTHER

OR

YOUR TEACHER?

HAVE A TINY DRAGON AS A SERVANT

OR

A LARGE DRAGON YOU CAN RIDE ON BUT IT HAS AN ANNOYING PERSONALITY?

WOULD YOU RATHER...

SLIP ON A BANANA PEEL

OR

TRIP OVER WHILE TRYING TO AVOID THE BANANA PEEL?

GIVE 20 PEOPLE $1,000 EACH

OR

ONE PERSON $20,000?

WOULD YOU RATHER...

RIDE IN A SMALL PLANE

OR

A LIMOUSINE?

BATTLE 20 ELEPHANTS THE SIZE OF A CHICKEN

OR

ONE CHICKEN THE SIZE OF AN ELEPHANT?

WOULD YOU RATHER...

BE REALLY HAIRY ALL OVER YOUR BODY

OR

NOT HAVE A SINGLE HAIR ON ANY PART OF YOUR BODY?

HAVE AN EASY JOB WORKING FOR SOMEONE ELSE

OR

WORK FOR YOURSELF BUT WORK INCREDIBLY HARD?

WOULD YOU RATHER...

BE STUCK IN A HURRICANE
FOR 1 DAY

OR

A BLIZZARD FOR 2 DAYS?

HAVE THE EYES OF A BAT

OR

THE WINGS OF A BAT?

WOULD YOU RATHER...

GO BOWLING WITH ALBERT EINSTEIN

OR

ABRAHAM LINCOLN?

WAKE UP WITH LION'S TEETH

OR

A TURTLE SHELL ON YOUR HEAD INSTEAD OF HAIR?

WOULD YOU RATHER...

LIVE THE NEXT 10 YEARS OF YOUR LIFE IN CHINA

OR

RUSSIA?

ALWAYS SCREAM YOUR NAME REALLY LOUDLY AS YOU ENTER THE ROOM

OR

ALWAYS WALK OUT BACKWARDS?

WOULD YOU RATHER...

HAVE A PET KANGAROO THAT CAN SPEAK ENGLISH

OR

A PET CAT THAT IS BIG ENOUGH TO RIDE?

WIN A 1-DAY SHOPPING SPREE TO ANY STORE

OR

A 2-WEEK VACATION TO ANY DESTINATION?

WOULD YOU RATHER...

NEVER BE ALLOWED TO WEAR UNDERWEAR AGAIN

OR

NEVER BE ALLOWED TO WEAR SHOES AGAIN?

WAKE UP WITH A BABY PANDA IN YOUR BED

OR

A BABY SLOTH IN YOUR BED?

WOULD YOU RATHER...

DRINK A CUP OF
SEA WATER

OR

A CUP OF CLEAN WATER OUT
OF YOUR TOILET?

HAVE FINGERS AS LONG
AS YOUR LEGS

OR

LEGS AS LONG AS
YOUR FINGERS?

WOULD YOU RATHER...

WEAR WET SOCKS

OR

WET UNDERWEAR?

YELL AT THE TOP OF YOUR VOICE EVERY TIME YOU SPOKE

OR

NEVER SPEAK AGAIN?

WOULD YOU RATHER...

ALWAYS BE DRESSED IN REALLY NICE CLOTHES

OR

ALWAYS WEAR YOUR PAJAMAS?

EAT 3 HOTDOGS

OR

A FULL TUB OF ICECREAM FOR LUNCH EVERY DAY FOR THE NEXT WEEK?

WOULD YOU RATHER...

BE ABLE TO TO READ THE MINDS OF BABIES

OR

SPEAK THE LANGUAGE OF BABIES AND TALK TO THEM?

LOSE YOUR SENSE OF SMELL FOR A YEAR

OR

SLEEP IN A GARBAGE DUMP FOR A MONTH?

WOULD YOU RATHER...

SWIM 3 TIMES FASTER THAN YOU CURRENTLY DO

OR

RUN 2 TIMES FASTER?

NEVER HAVE ANY HOMEWORK

OR

BE PAID $3 PER HOUR FOR DOING YOUR HOMEWORK?

WOULD YOU RATHER...

NEVER BE ABLE TO LIE EVER AGAIN

OR

ONLY BE ABLE TO LIE IF YOU YELL REALLY LOUDLY?

HAVE A PET HORSE YOU CAN SHOW YOUR FRIENDS

OR

A PET FLYING UNICORN THAT YOU CAN NEVER TALK ABOUT OR SHOW ANYONE?

WOULD YOU RATHER...

GIVE UP YOUR CELL PHONE FOR A MONTH

OR

WEAR A USED, SMELLY DIAPER AS A HAT FOR A WEEK?

HAVE A TWO-BEDROOM APARTMENT IN A BIG CITY

OR

A MANSION IN THE COUNTRYSIDE?

WOULD YOU RATHER...

BE COMPLETELY BALD

OR

HAVE HAIR THAT IS SO LONG IT DRAGS ON THE FLOOR?

HAVE A TAIL THAT CAN'T GRAB THINGS

OR

WINGS THAT CAN'T FLY?

WOULD YOU RATHER...

BE ALLERGIC TO CANDY

OR

ALLERGIC TO BACON?

GO TO A DOCTOR'S APPOINTMENT

OR

A DENTIST APPOINTMENT?

WOULD YOU RATHER...

HAVE A SMALL CHILD WET THEIR PANTS WHILE SITTING ON YOUR LAP

OR

YOU WET YOUR OWN PANTS WHILE IN CLASS?

HAVE AN EXTRA EYE ON YOUR FOREHEAD

OR

AN EXTRA EYE ON THE BACK OF YOUR HEAD?

WOULD YOU RATHER...

HAVE HANDS INSTEAD OF FEET

OR

FEET INSTEAD OF HANDS?

HAVE 2 HEADS AND BE AN ABSOLUTE GENIUS

OR

ONE HEAD AND BE OF AVERAGE INTELLIGENCE?

WOULD YOU RATHER...

EAT ONLY REALLY HEALTHY SMOOTHIES FOR EVERY MEAL

OR

FAST FOOD FOR EVERY MEAL FOR THE NEXT YEAR?

HAVE A PET WORM THAT LIVED IN YOUR NOSE

OR

A PET FLY THAT LIVED IN YOUR EAR?

WOULD YOU RATHER...

HAVE A HORRIBLE SHORT-TERM MEMORY

OR

A HORRIBLE LONG-TERM MEMORY?

WATCH NETFLIX ALL WEEKEND

OR

DISNEY+ ALL WEEKEND?

WOULD YOU RATHER...

SLEEP IN A SMALL SUITCASE

OR

SLEEP ON PINE CONES?

INSTANTLY BECOME A GROWN UP

OR

STAY THE AGE YOU ARE NOW FOR ANOTHER TWO YEARS?

WOULD YOU RATHER...

THAT IT IS ALWAYS SUMMER ALL YEAR LONG

OR

THAT WE HAVE THE FOUR SEASONS LIKE WE DO NOW?

BE PRANKED BY YOUR FRIENDS

OR

BE A WELL KNOWN PRANKSTER?

WOULD YOU RATHER...

GET BITTEN BY A SPIDER ONCE A MONTH FOR A YEAR

OR

STUNG BY A BEE ONCE A DAY FOR A YEAR?

SPEND A WEEK AT HOGWARTS WITH HARRY POTTER

OR

GET TO TRAVEL ON THE MILLENNIUM FALCON WITH CHEWBACCA?

WOULD YOU RATHER...

LIVE IN A HOUSE FULL
OF DOGS

OR

A HOUSE FULL OF CATS?

EAT A SMALL CAN OF
CAT FOOD

OR

EAT TWO ROTTEN
TOMATOES?

WOULD YOU RATHER...

WRESTLE A GIANT SNAKE

OR

WRESTLE A GIANT SPIDER?

GO ON ONE BIG VACATION FOR 2 MONTHS

OR

4 SMALL VACATIONS OF ONE WEEK EACH?

WOULD YOU RATHER...

EAT MASHED BANANA WITH GARLIC

OR

A HOTDOG MADE WITH ONIONS?

LIVE COMPLETELY ALONE FOREVER

OR

FACE YOUR BIGGEST FEAR ONCE A MONTH?

WOULD YOU RATHER...

SLEEP IN A GARBAGE BIN
FOR A WEEK

OR

IN A PIGSTY FOR
2 NIGHTS?

BE THE FUNNIEST KID
AT SCHOOL

OR

THE SMARTEST KID
AT SCHOOL?

WOULD YOU RATHER...

GIVE A SPEECH IN FRONT
OF 200 PEOPLE

OR

DO A DANCE IN FRONT
OF 200 PEOPLE?

HAVE ALL TRAFFIC LIGHTS YOU
APPROACH TURN GREEN

OR

NEVER HAVE TO STAND
IN LINE AGAIN?

WOULD YOU RATHER...

GO SWIMMING IN A RIVER OF HOT CHOCOLATE

OR

DIVE INTO A POOL OF MELTED ICE CREAM?

HAVE ONE EXTRA ARM

OR

ONE EXTRA LEG?

WOULD YOU RATHER...

SLEEP IN YOUR PARENTS' BED EVERY NIGHT

OR

CRY UNCONTROLLABLY EVERY TIME SOMEONE TELLS YOU A JOKE?

YOUR ONLY MODE OF TRANSPORTATION BE A DONKEY

OR

A GIRAFFE?

WOULD YOU RATHER...

TRAIN A DINOSAUR SIZED CHICKEN

OR

TRAIN A CHICKEN SIZED DINOSAUR?

BE ABLE TO TALK TO ALL ANIMALS

OR

BE AN ANIMAL OF YOUR CHOICE?

WOULD YOU RATHER...

GIVE YOUR OWN SECRET HANDSHAKE

OR

A HIGH FIVE?

COMMUNICATE ONLY USING SIGN LANGUAGE

OR

YELL REALLY LOUDLY WHENEVER YOU TALKED?

WOULD YOU RATHER...

BE TRAPPED FOR A DAY IN A ROOM FULL OF LIZARDS

OR

A ROOM FULL OF SKUNKS?

HAVE 1,000 COCKROACHES IN YOUR BEDROOM

OR

HAVE A BATH WITH 1,000 WRIGGLING WORMS?

WOULD YOU RATHER...

HAVE TO LAUGH OUT LOUD
EVERY TIME YOU TYPE LOL

OR

ALWAYS REPLICATE THE FACE
OF ANY EMOJI YOU USE?

SMELL LIKE A SKUNK
FOR A WEEK

OR

SMELL LIKE ROTTEN EGGS
FOR A MONTH?

WOULD YOU RATHER...

LOSE YOUR CELL PHONE

OR

LOSE YOUR KEYS?

BE ABLE TO READ ANY
PERSON'S MIND

OR

BE ABLE TO LOOK INTO
THE FUTURE?

WOULD YOU RATHER...

RIDE ON THE BACK OF A T-REX

OR

FLY ON THE BACK OF A PTERODACTYL?

LIVE IN A HOUSE ON THE BEACH

OR

LIVE IN A HIGH TECH APARTMENT WITH ALL THE LATEST GADGETS?

WOULD YOU RATHER...

SING LOUDLY IN THE SHOWER

OR

WHILE YOU ARE ON THE TOILET SEAT?

BE ABLE TO SEE THROUGH SOLID WALLS

OR

HEAR PEOPLE TALKING A MILE AWAY?

WOULD YOU RATHER...

BE A MASTER AT
ORIGAMI

OR

A MASTER OF SLEIGHT OF
HAND MAGIC?

BE ABLE TO JUMP 10 FEET
IN THE AIR

OR

HOLD YOUR BREATH
UNDERWATER FOR 10 MINUTES?

WOULD YOU RATHER...

HAVE A THREE FEET LONG NECK

OR

EARS AS BIG AS AN ELEPHANT?

LIVE ON THE BEACH

OR

IN A CABIN IN THE WOODS?

WOULD YOU RATHER...

BE THE EVIL MOVIE CHARACTER
WHO ALWAYS WINS

OR

THE GOOD MOVIE CHARACTER
WHO ALWAYS LOSES?

SPEAK IN THE VOICE
OF YODA

OR

DARTH VADER?

WOULD YOU RATHER...

HAVE THREE TEETH
PULLED OUT

OR

HAVE TO BE BEST FRIENDS
WITH YOUR WORST ENEMY?

SEE A MOSQUITO THE SIZE
OF A BEAR

OR

A BEAR THE SIZE OF A
MOSQUITO?

WOULD YOU RATHER...

WEAR REALLY UNCOMFORTABLE SHOES FOR AN HOUR

OR

JEANS THAT WERE 2 SIZES TOO SMALL FOR AN HOUR?

EAT A KETCHUP SANDWICH

OR

A CHILLI SAUCE SANDWICH?

WOULD YOU RATHER...

EAT ONE LEMON

OR

10 ORANGES?

ALWAYS TALK IN RHYMES

OR

ALWAYS SING INSTEAD OF SPEAKING?

WOULD YOU RATHER...

HAVE A SNOWBALL FIGHT

OR

A WATER BALLOON FIGHT?

BE LOST IN A BAD PART OF TOWN

OR

LOST IN THE FOREST?

WOULD YOU RATHER...

BE A POLICE OFFICER WITH A SQUEAKY VOICE

OR

A POLICE OFFICER WITH THE APPEARANCE OF A 12 YEAR OLD?

HAVE A CLONE OF YOU THAT DOES YOUR HOMEWORK

OR

HYPNOTIZE YOUR TEACHER SO YOU DON'T GET ANY HOMEWORK?

WOULD YOU RATHER...

GO ON A VACATION
WITH YOUR FAMILY

OR

STAY HOME WITH
YOUR FRIENDS?

TOUCH A PERSON AND HEAL
ANY DISEASE IN THEIR BODY

OR

TOUCH YOURSELF AND
LIVE FOREVER?

WOULD YOU RATHER...

HAVE AN UNLIMITED SUPPLY OF HOTDOGS

OR

AN UNLIMITED SUPPLY OF PIZZA?

HAVE CHRISTMAS DAY WHERE IT'S COLD AND SNOWING

OR

ON A SUNNY DAY AT THE BEACH?

WOULD YOU RATHER...

HAVE BRIGHT SUNSHINE 24 HOURS A DAY FOR A YEAR

OR

BE DARK WITH A FULL MOON FOR A YEAR?

DRINK 15 GLASSES OF WATER IN A ROW

OR

DRINK ONE GLASS OF SOY SAUCE?

WOULD YOU RATHER...

HAVE UNLIMITED SUSHI
FOR LIFE

OR

UNLIMITED TACOS
FOR LIFE?

EAT A BREAKFAST OF FRIED
SPINACH ON TOAST

OR

ROAST CARROTS WITH
GRAVY?

WOULD YOU RATHER...

LIVE UNDER A SKY WITH NO STARS AT NIGHT

OR

NO CLOUDS DURING THE DAY?

LEARN SIGN LANGUAGE

OR

LEARN HOW TO LIP READ?

WOULD YOU RATHER...

BE ABLE TO TALK
TO DOGS

OR

CATS?

LIVE IN A HOUSE MADE OF
VEGETABLES

OR

A HOUSE MADE OF
MEAT?

WOULD YOU RATHER...

HAVE A SELF DRIVING CAR THAT CAN DRIVE ANYWHERE

OR

A SELF DRIVING BOAT THAT CAN SAIL ANYWHERE?

BE A MERMAID WITH THE HEAD OF A DOLPHIN

OR

A DOLPHIN WITH THE HEAD OF A MERMAID?

WOULD YOU RATHER...

BE A ROBOT THAT COULD
LIVE FOREVER

OR

A HUMAN WHO LIVES FOR
80 YEARS?

KISS A RAT

OR

HUG A HEDGEHOG?

WOULD YOU RATHER...

HAVE A SMELLY STAIN ON YOUR JEANS AND NOT NOTICE

OR

A HOLE IN YOUR JEANS AND NOT NOTICE?

BE BEST FRIENDS WITH THE PRESIDENT

OR

BEST FRIENDS WITH A FAMOUS ACTOR?

WOULD YOU RATHER...

COOK EVERY MEAL FOR A YEAR

OR

ONLY EAT FAST FOOD FOR A YEAR?

CONTROL YOUR DREAMS AS YOU ARE DREAMING

OR

BE ABLE TO WATCH YOUR DREAMS ON TV THE NEXT DAY?

WOULD YOU RATHER...

EAT BRUSSEL SPROUTS FOR
EVERY MEAL

OR

LIVE IN THE WILDERNESS FOR
THE REST OF YOUR LIFE?

HAVE SUPER LONG
EXTENDING LEGS

OR

HAVE SUPER LONG
EXTENDING ARMS?

WOULD YOU RATHER...

HAVE TWO TONGUES

OR

A FORKED TONGUE LIKE A SNAKE?

GET CHASED BY ONE ANGRY LLAMA

OR

12 ANGRY SQUIRRELS?

WOULD YOU RATHER...

BECOME FIVE YEARS OLDER

OR

BECOME TWO YEARS YOUNGER?

BE ABLE TO READ THE MIND OF YOUR PET

OR

HAVE YOUR PET SPEAK AND UNDERSTAND ENGLISH?

WOULD YOU RATHER...

RIDE IN A GIANT KANGAROO'S POUCH

OR

ON THE BACK OF A GIANT EAGLE?

HAVE ONE HUGE EYEBROW ACROSS YOUR FOREHEAD

OR

NO EYEBROWS AT ALL?

WOULD YOU RATHER...

RIDE A BULL AT THE RODEO FOR 30 SECONDS

OR

SWIM WITH A SHARK FOR 10 SECONDS?

BE ABLE TO CONTROL WATER IN ANY FORM

OR

THE WIND?

WOULD YOU RATHER...

HAVE A SCARY SMILE THAT MAKES SMALL CHILDREN CRY

OR

A REALLY LOUD LAUGH THAT CAN DEAFEN PEOPLE?

HAVE A BABY THROW UP ON YOU

OR

YOU THROW UP ON A BABY?

WOULD YOU RATHER...

DRINK ALL YOUR FOOD FROM A BABY BOTTLE

OR

WEAR VISIBLE DIAPERS FOR THE REST OF YOUR LIFE?

BE A CHARACTER IN YOUR FAVORITE TV SHOW

OR

A CHARACTER IN YOUR FAVORITE BOOK?

WOULD YOU RATHER...

PLAY BASKETBALL AT THE OLYMPICS

OR

PLAY BASKETBALL FOR THE LA LAKERS?

BE COMPLETELY ALONE FOR 5 YEARS

OR

BE SURROUNDED BY PEOPLE AND NEVER BE ALONE FOR 5 YEARS?

WOULD YOU RATHER...

HAVE 3 INCH LONG
NOSE HAIRS

OR

3 INCH LONG EAR
HAIRS?

BRUSH YOUR TEETH WITH
YOUR FINGERS

OR

LET SOMEONE ELSE BRUSH YOUR
TEETH WITH THEIR FINGERS?

WOULD YOU RATHER...

LIVE IN THE MINECRAFT WORLD

OR

THE STAR WARS WORLD?

BE COMPLETELY INVISIBLE FOR ONE DAY

OR

BE ABLE TO FLY FOR ONE DAY?

WOULD YOU RATHER...

THAT 5% OF THE POPULATION CAN READ MINDS

OR

5% OF THE POPULATION CAN MOVE THINGS WITH THEIR MIND?

BE ABLE TO CHANGE COLOR TO CAMOUFLAGE YOURSELF

OR

GROW FIFTEEN FEET TALLER AND SHRINK BACK DOWN WHENEVER YOU WANTED?

WOULD YOU RATHER...

WEAR HIGH HEELS

OR

WEAR FLIP FLOPS?

EAT A MONTH'S WORTH OF PIZZA IN ONE NIGHT

OR

NEVER EAT PIZZA AGAIN?

WOULD YOU RATHER...

DRIVE ALL OVER THE COUNTRY FOR A YEAR

OR

GO TO YOUR ONE FAVORITE HOLIDAY SPOT FOR A YEAR?

HAVE THE ABILITY TO TELEPORT ANYWHERE

OR

BE ABLE TO CREATE LEGAL 5 DOLLAR BILLS BY CLAPPING?

WOULD YOU RATHER...

DRINK A GLASS OF MAYONNAISE
IN ONE SITTING

OR

USE MAYONNAISE AS
TOOTHPASTE FOR THE NEXT
3 WEEKS?

WEAR YOUR UNDERWEAR ON
YOUR HEAD AS A HAT

OR

YOUR DAD'S UNDERWEAR ON
YOUR HEAD WHEN YOU
MEET THE PRESIDENT?

WOULD YOU RATHER...

WIN $100,000

OR

HAVE YOUR BEST FRIEND WIN $1,000,000?

EAT A ROTTEN BANANA

OR

EAT A CUP FULL OF GRASS?

WOULD YOU RATHER...

HAVE A SHOWER THAT KEEPS YOU CLEAN FOR 7 DAYS

OR

HAVE A BED THAT GIVES YOU A FULL NIGHT'S REST IN 1 HOUR?

BRUSH YOUR TEETH WITH HOT MUSTARD

OR

KETCHUP?

WOULD YOU RATHER...

BE AN AVERAGE TENNIS PLAYER

OR

WIN OLYMPIC GOLD IN TABLE TENNIS?

HAVE THE SUN SET AT 4PM EVERY DAY

OR

11PM EVERY NIGHT?

WOULD YOU RATHER...

NEVER BE ABLE TO USE A TOUCHSCREEN

OR

NEVER BE ABLE TO USE A KEYBOARD AND MOUSE?

WALK FOR 3 MILES BAREFOOT

OR

LAY STILL ON THE PAVEMENT FOR 3 HOURS?

WOULD YOU RATHER...

GO TO AN ACTION MOVIE WITH YOUR BEST FRIEND

OR

YOUR PARENTS?

HAVE A MASSIVE HEAD COMPARED TO YOUR BODY

OR

MASSIVE EYES COMPARED TO YOUR HEAD?

WOULD YOU RATHER...

SPEAK 10 DIFFERENT LANGUAGES

OR

ONLY YOUR CURRENT LANGUAGE?

HAVE A MAGIC WAND

OR

A LIGHTSABER?

WOULD YOU RATHER...

PROVE THAT THE EARTH
IS HOLLOW

OR

THAT THE EARTH IS FLAT?

VISIT THE MOON

OR

VISIT MARS?

WOULD YOU RATHER...

BE LOST IN THE WOODS
AT NIGHT

OR

STUCK IN A HAUNTED HOUSE
AT NIGHT?

HAVE A NEVER-ENDING SUPPLY
OF CHOCOLATE

OR

A NEVER-ENDING SUPPLY OF
CHEESEBURGERS?

WOULD YOU RATHER?

EWW! YUCK! GROSS!

This way to crazy, ridiculous and downright hilarious 'Would You Rathers?!'

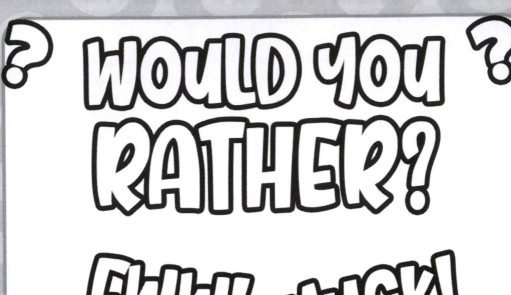

WARNING!

These are Eww! These are Yuck! These are Gross! And they are really funny! Laughter awaits!

WOULD YOU RATHER...

KISS A DEAD RAT

OR

EAT AN EARWIG?

LICK YOUR BEST FRIEND'S EYEBALL

OR

EAT A ROTTEN TOMATO?

WOULD YOU RATHER...

HAVE A BATH IN WARM VOMIT

OR

SLEEP UNDER A PILE OF USED BABY DIAPERS?

HAVE YOUR FARTS SMELL LIKE KFC

OR

APPLE PIE?

WOULD YOU RATHER...

LICK THE ARMPIT OF A SWEATY HIKER

OR

LICK THE EARWAX OF AN OLD MAN?

HAVE A JOB PICKING UP LLAMA POOP

OR

ELEPHANT POOP?

WOULD YOU RATHER...

VOMIT ON YOUR GRANDPA

OR

HAVE YOUR GRANDPA VOMIT ON YOU?

HAVE YOUR FARTS SOUND LIKE A CAR HORN

OR

A LION ROARING?

WOULD YOU RATHER...

CLEAN THE TOILET WITH YOUR TONGUE

OR

DRINK A CUP OF TOILET WATER?

A JOB POPPING STRANGERS' PIMPLES

OR

PICKING THEIR NOSE AND LICKING THEIR BOOGERS?

WOULD YOU RATHER...

EAT A BOWL OF DEAD INSECTS

OR

A PIECE OF RAW MEAT?

3 HUGE SPIDERS CRAWL ON YOUR HEAD

OR

HAVE LOTS OF LITTLE BABY SPIDERS COME OUT OF YOUR PIMPLE?

WOULD YOU RATHER...

BURP IN FRONT OF YOUR TEACHER

OR

FART LOUDLY ON A FIRST DATE?

BREATHE IN A BAG OF SMELLY FARTS

OR

EAT A BOWL OF ROTTEN RAW EGGS?

WOULD YOU RATHER...

SNIFF A CAT'S BUTT

OR

SNIFF A DOG'S BUTT?

EAT A SMALL CAN OF
CAT FOOD

OR

4 ROTTEN APPLES?

WOULD YOU RATHER...

ACCIDENTALLY FART REALLY LOUD IN PUBLIC

OR

ACCIDENTALLY PEE YOURSELF IN PUBLIC?

YOUR FRIEND'S BROTHER BARFED ON YOUR BED

OR

A HAPPY, ELDERLY GENTLEMAN DID A POOP ON YOUR PORCH?

WOULD YOU RATHER...

FART OUT OF BOTH EARS AT ONCE

OR

BE ABLE TO CONTROL WHICH EAR YOU FARTED OUT OF?

RECEIVE A GIFT OF A JAR OF PICKLED EYEBALLS

OR

A GIFT-WRAPPED BOX OF DRIED ANIMAL POOPS?

THANKS A BUNCH!

For reading our book!
We hope you have enjoyed these
'WOULD YOU RATHER?'
scenarios as much as we did as we were
putting this book together.
If you could possibly leave a review of our
book we would really appreciate it. ☺

To see all our latest books or leave a review
just go to
RatherFunnyPress.com
Once again, thanks so much for reading!

P.S. If you enjoyed the bonus chapter,
EWW! YUCK! GROSS!
you can always check out our brand new book,

WOULD YOU RATHER?
EWW! YUCK! GROSS!
for hundreds of brand new, crazy and ridiculous
scenarios that are sure to get the kids rolling on the
floor with laughter!
Just go to:
RatherFunnyPress.com
Thanks again! ☺

YOUR FREE SURPRISE GIFT!

To grab your free copy of this brand new, hilarious Joke Book, just go to:

go.RatherFunnyPress.com

Enjoy!

RatherFunnyPress.com